Marta's Magnets

by Wendy Pfeffer
illustrated by Gail Piazza

Silver Press

Parsippany, New Jersey

For my mother and father,
Who encouraged me to learn about everything,
including magnets.

With thanks to Ruth Ann van Veenendaal and her
third graders for reviewing the manuscript and
sharing their experiences with me.

–Wendy Pfeffer

For Bob and Sue,
And a special thanks to the eight children that
helped make the pictures come alive.

–Gail Piazza

Published by Silver Press,
a division of Simon & Schuster
299 Jefferson Road, Parsippany, New Jersey 07054

Designed by JP Design Associates

Manufactured in the United States of America

10 9 8 7 6 5 4 3

Library of Congress Cataloging-in-Publication Data
Pfeffer, Wendy, 1929–
    Marta's magnets/by Wendy Pfeffer; illustrated by Gail
Piazza.   p. cm.
    Summary: Marta's sister Rosa calls her magnet collection
junk, but Marta's magnets help her make friends in her new
home and help her retrieve a lost key for Rosa's new friend.
    [1. Magnets—Fiction. 2. Friendship—Fiction. 3. Hispanic
Americans—Fiction.] I. Piazza, Gail, 1956–   ill. II. Title.
PZ7.P448556Mar 1995
[E]—dc20 94-37223   CIP   AC
ISBN 0-382-24930-5 (LSB)   ISBN 0-382-24931-3 (JHC)
ISBN 0-382-24932-1 (S/C)

Marta loved to collect things. She collected sticks
and stones, cards and cardboard, little boxes, big
boxes, and…well, just about anything. So, when
Marta's family moved, her collections moved, too…
right into the room Marta shared with her older
sister, Rosa.

Rosa's side of the room was sparkling clean. Marta's wasn't. Her bed was covered with crepe paper from broken-open piñatas. Her mirror was hidden by chains made from gum wrappers. On her desk sat a ball of string, the size of a soccer ball, and a shoe box full of magnets.

Colleen, Rosa's new friend who lived across the hall,
peeked into the bedroom. "What a lot of junk,"
she said.

"Yeah!" agreed Rosa.

"My collections are not junk. They're my treasures,"
said Marta, sorting through her magnets, trying to
ignore Rosa and Colleen.

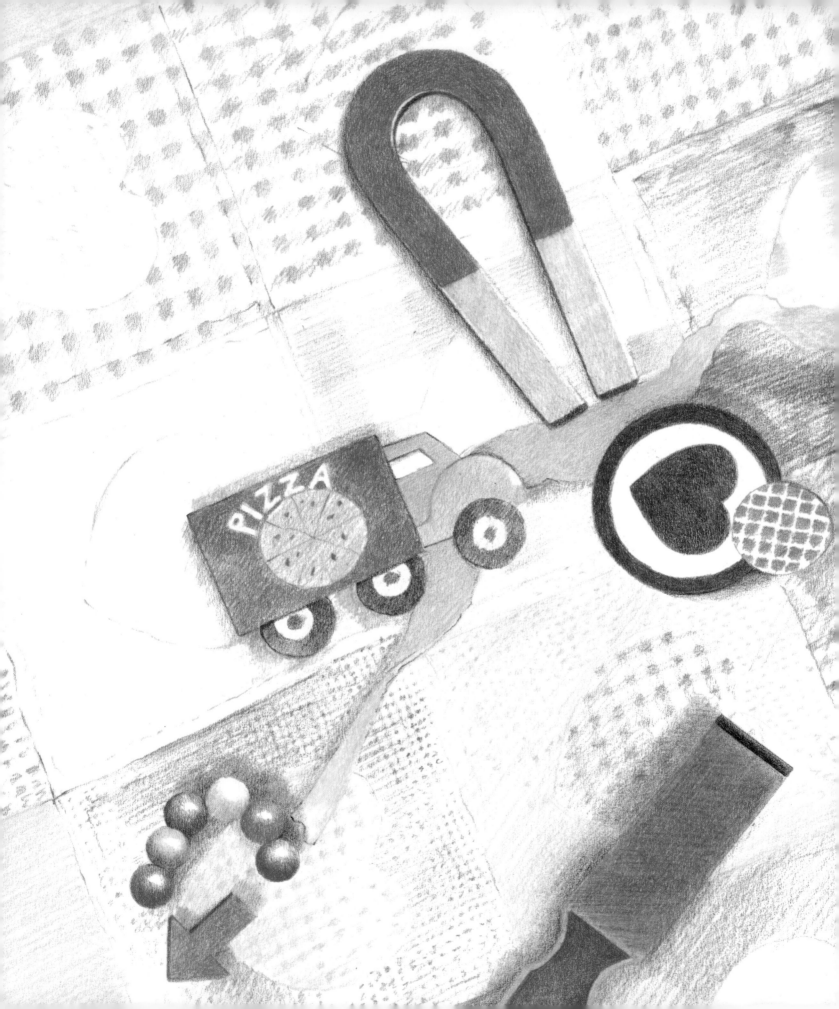

Marta found the bar magnets from a birthday grab
bag. She saw the magnets she'd cut from the
bottom of an old shower curtain. And she picked
up the horseshoe magnet that she had saved from
an old science kit. But Marta's favorite was the
truck-shaped magnet a pizza delivery boy had
given her. She stuck it in her pocket.

In the kitchen Marta poured herself some juice
from the refrigerator. As she drank, she kept
sticking her truck magnet on the door and
peeling it off.

"More junk, Marta?" said Rosa, sharing her
sunflower seeds with Colleen.

"I don't call your bottles of nail polish and glitter
junk," Marta said, angrily stomping into her room.

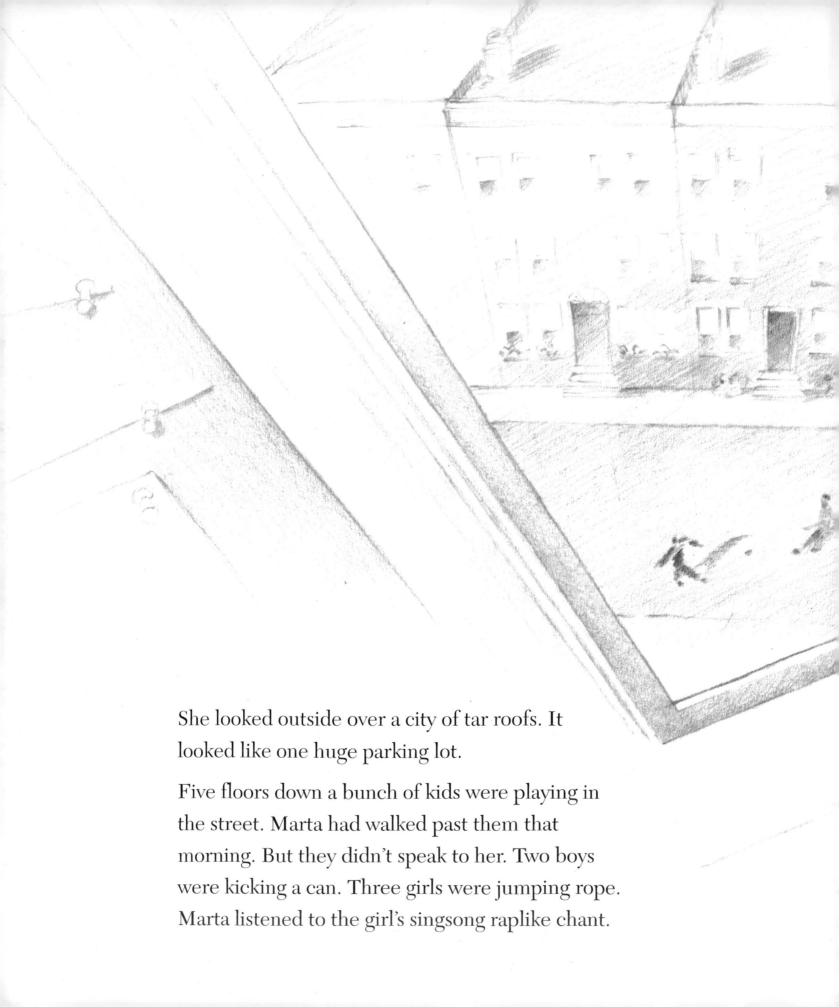

She looked outside over a city of tar roofs. It looked like one huge parking lot.

Five floors down a bunch of kids were playing in the street. Marta had walked past them that morning. But they didn't speak to her. Two boys were kicking a can. Three girls were jumping rope. Marta listened to the girl's singsong raplike chant.

"One potato, two potato, three potato, four.
Jump to the window. Jump to the door.
Five potato, six potato, seven potato, eight.
Jump to the garden. Jump to the gate."

Grabbing her magnets, Marta bounced down five flights of stairs and ran out the door. "Hey, guys!" she called. "My name's Marta."

The boys kept kicking the can. The girls kept jumping rope.

Marta stuck one of her magnets on an iron railing,
another on a fire hydrant, and a third on a traffic sign.

The kids stopped playing. "What're you doing?" asked the taller boy.

"Sticking magnets on things," said Marta. "This truck stuck on my refrigerator door. Want to try a magnet?" she added, offering one to each kid.

"Sure," said the tall boy, "I'm Marshall."

"My name's Stevie," said the other boy. "Over there is Kim. She doesn't talk much."

Kim peeked over her glasses. She rubbed the smooth edges of the magnet Marta handed her and smiled.

One of the girls put down her ends of the rope.
"My name's Tanya, and this is Vanya," she said.
"We're twins."

Vanya stuck her magnet in her pocket. "Want to
jump rope?" she asked.

"Sure!" said Marta, as Tanya began to chant,

"One potato, two potato, three potato, four.
A truck got stuck on Marta's door.
Five potato, six potato, seven potato, eight.
Maybe it'll stick on the garden gate."

Marta joined in. She loved the slip-slap, slip-slap
rhythm of the rope skipping on the sidewalk. She
jumped until Stevie yelled, "This magnet stuck to
the air conditioner."

Marshall waved his magnet. "Magnets attract a lot
of things. See, mine sticks to this old steel can."

In a few minutes excited voices seemed to drift up
and bounce off the brick row houses.

"This magnet doesn't stick to my soda can."

"Hey, the magnet stuck to the key in my pocket."

"Mine doesn't stick to my key."

"This one sticks to the nail in the door, but not
the door."

Then a voice, like a whisper, floated among
the others.

"This magnet doesn't stick to my glasses," said Kim.

Marta smiled. Her magnets were special—they
attracted friends, and they made Kim speak.

Marta turned toward Rosa and Colleen. She hoped they saw her five new friends. But Rosa was on her hands and knees, and Colleen was crying. Marta ran over to them.

"Colleen lost her key ring down this grating," said Rosa. "She can't get into her apartment without her key. She can't take the stew out of the freezer. Dinner won't be on time. Her mom will be late for night school. And…"

"I have an idea," said Marta. She ran into her building and climbed the stairs.

The smell of chicken soup drifted over the first floor. Bright colors decorated the second floor walls. Bicycles and hockey sticks filled the third floor hall. A baby crying told Marta she must be on the fourth floor. And the fifth floor smelled like home. An apartment building is a collection, too…of different people. Marta ran into her apartment and came out carrying her ball of string.

On the sidewalk all the kids were looking down the grating. Marta knelt next to Rosa. She looked down, too. She saw nothing. Suddenly a ray of sunlight shone on a tiny object. It glistened. The key! Something else glistened. Water! Oh, no! thought Marta. Maybe my magnet won't work in water.

Marta sat up. She tied the string around her magnet. She lowered it through the grating until it was right…on…the…key.

Carefully she pulled the string up. The magnet was empty. She tried once more. Again, no key! Then she remembered. Marshall's magnet didn't attract his key. That could be the problem. Or water could be the problem. Marta lowered the magnet. Again, no key!

The next time she lowered the magnet she aimed
at the key ring. But that was in the water, too. The
magnet swayed back and forth over the key ring.
Suddenly—Wham!—they connected. Inch by inch
she pulled the string up.

"There's the key ring." yelled Rosa. "It's dangling from the magnet."

"So are four paper clips," Marta said. "My magnet is a collector, too."

Colleen grabbed the key ring and gave Marta a big hug. "Hooray for Marta's magnet!" the kids yelled.

Marta still collects things. She keeps keys in see-through boxes, hangs paper-clip chains beside the gum-wrapper chains on her mirror, and loves to stick magnets of every size, shape, and color on her old iron bed.

Marta's magnets *must* be special because Rosa and Colleen *never* again called Marta's collections junk.

Making a Refrigerator Magnet

1. Ask an adult to help you collect these things.

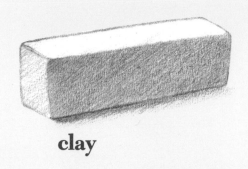
clay

glue

paint

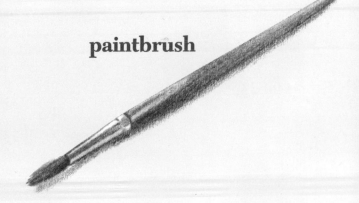
paintbrush

clear nail polish

small flat magnet

2. Mold the clay into any shape you want . . . maybe a pizza truck like Marta's. Keep the back flat.

3. Let the clay harden overnight.

4. Paint your creation. Let the paint dry.

5. Brush on clear nail polish to keep the paint bright.

6. Glue a small magnet on the back. Let the glue dry.

7. Proudly place your magnet on the refrigerator.